For Judy Wachs –
The life and soul of the party.

Massive thanks to Janetta Otter-Barry, Gemma Rochelle
and the rest of the Frances Lincoln crew, for believing
in this book and making it happen.

Dan and the Mudman copyright © Frances Lincoln Limited 2008
Text copyright © Jonny Zucker 2008

First published in Great Britain in 2008 and the USA in 2009 by
Frances Lincoln Children's Books, 4 Torriano Mews,
Torriano Avenue, London NW5 2RZ
www.franceslincoln.com

First paperback edition 2009

British Library Cataloguing in Publication Data available on request

ISBN 978-1-84507-673-3

Set in AGaramond

Printed in China

1 3 5 7 9 8 6 4 2

Dan and the Mudman

Jonny Zucker

FRANCES LINCOLN
CHILDREN'S BOOKS

MONDAY

Dan Bernstein had only been at Oakridge School for two and a half hours but he was already planning his escape.

He had to get out of here – and fast.

He stared at his reflection in the rain-splattered classroom window.

A boy with a buzz haircut, large, oval brown eyes, a tiny scar above his left eyebrow, and thin, unsmiling lips, stared back.

Dan took a quick sideways glance at Lucy Osbourne, the girl he'd been told to sit next to. She had blonde hair scraped back into a ponytail, bright blue eyes and a button nose. In between bouts of writing in her English book, she'd been filling Dan in about all of his new classmates; who were the friendly ones, who were the weird ones and who were the ones to avoid at all costs.

Dan looked down at the accusing blank pages in

his English book and cursed his mum for the ten millionth time. Why had she gone and applied for that stupid job as nursing manager in a big hospital up north? She'd said that she probably wouldn't get it, but then she breezed through the interview. A week later, she and Dad told him they were leaving London to move up to Wareham, where Mum's new job was based.

"It's the answer to all our money worries," Dad had declared. "It'll give us a real chance to pay off our debts."

Dan hadn't taken the news very well; in fact he'd completely flipped.

"YOU CAN'T DO THIS!" he shouted. "Mum will just have to get a promotion down here. You can't sell the house. There's NO WAY I'm leaving my school, or my mates."

But his parents had made up their minds and no matter how hard Dan argued, pleaded, and cajoled, it was a done deal. They sold the house and a month later, in the last week of August, the three of them drove up the motorway with all their possessions stuffed into their battered roof-box.

Dan's worst fears were confirmed on arrival.

Wareham's town centre looked very uninviting. It was a drab and dull mesh of interconnecting slabs of grey stones; and its shops were rubbish.

Their new road looked just as unappealing. It was long and packed with small, white terraced houses. It looked like it had been made from a kit. The neighbours on both sides were elderly couples. In the Bernsteins' road in London, kids always played out on the streets, but here, you only saw the odd blurred figure, whizzing past on a bike. Dan had three days to settle in before the start of the autumn term at Oakridge. He'd spent the whole time moping up in his bedroom.

The voice of his new teacher, Miss Foxton, brought him crashing back to earth. She was tall and slim with high cheekbones and shiny hazel eyes.

"Ok, listen," she said.

Pens were put down, papers were shuffled and then all eyes turned to face her.

"As your first big project of the year," she

announced, "I want all of you to prepare a presentation. This can be on any subject you like and you may use any medium you like to present it – within reason of course. You will make this presentation to the rest of the class two weeks from today."

There was an outbreak of whispering in the class.

"Brilliant!" Lucy exclaimed. "I'm going to make a film with my dad's camcorder!"

Lucy's enthusiasm contrasted sharply with Dan's feeling of dread.

A presentation? In front of the whole class?

That was the last thing he needed. All he wanted to do was keep his head down and save enough money to go back to London. He really wasn't in the mood for any stupid presentation.

Dan ate his packed lunch with Lucy in the canteen. She told him she wanted to be a professional photographer and showed him some of the wildlife pictures she'd taken on a recent visit to the local zoo. They were pretty impressive. She asked Dan about his future plans.

"Running," he replied between mouthfuls of sandwich. "I do the longer races – you know, cross-country, five-thousand-metre races, that kind of thing."

"Sounds amazing," Lucy smiled. "Do you train all the time?"

Dan blew out his cheeks. "I'm not doing that much at the minute," he replied.

Normally Dan went running at least once a day, but since his parents had announced the move, he'd hardly been out all. His spirits were so deflated that he didn't feel like doing anything really – especially not donning a tracksuit and going out in the wind and the rain.

Dan had quickly decided that Lucy was OK. She wasn't ever going replace his mates back home, but it was good to have someone to talk to on your first day, instead of sitting by yourself like a friendless geek.

After school, Lucy walked most of the way home with him. The sky was overcast and pockets of rain drizzled down. Lucy only lived a couple of streets away. He said goodbye to her and tramped the rest of the way home.

***

"How was your first day at Oakridge?" asked Dad, ladling pasta on to three plates in the kitchen. Dan muttered under his breath and threw his coat down on to the back of a chair.

Dan's father was six foot two. He had a wiry body, kind hazel eyes and a thin covering of salt and pepper hair. He was in a good mood. He was an electrician and that afternoon he'd been offered a three-month contract to fit out a chain of jewellery stores.

A couple of minutes later Mum walked in. She was short and slim with deep blue eyes and a long, friendly face. It was only her third day at the new job but already she looked exhausted.

"How was your first day, babe?" she asked, putting a hand on Dan's shoulder.

Dan flicked her hand away, said nothing and took his place at the table. He'd been giving his parents the silent treatment ever since they'd announced they were selling the house and moving to Wareham. When he wasn't being silent he was edgy and angry.

"Come on, love," smiled Mum. "We know how hard this is for you, but at least tell us a little bit about Oakridge."

Dan picked up a fork and threw it back down on to the table. "There's nothing to tell,' he snarled. "I hate the school. I hate the town. I hate this house!"

"Hey," said Dad, his eyes pools of concern, "it will turn out OK, I'm telling you. You'll be happy up here."

"No!" Dan shouted. "I'm NEVER going to be happy here!"

He pushed his uneaten plate of food across the table and stormed out of the kitchen. He stamped upstairs, flung open his bedroom door and threw himself down on his bed.

What was it with his parents? When would they get it into their stupid heads, that they'd ruined his life?

TUESDAY

At breakfast the next morning, Dan's parents gave him a wide berth. He read an old running magazine over his cornflakes, got his stuff together and left the house without saying goodbye. He'd spotted the anxious glances they'd exchanged across the kitchen table, but that was their problem. If they felt guilty, they'd have to deal with it.

He'd just turned the corner at the end of his road, when he spied Lucy, sitting on a low brick wall in front of a house.

"I thought I'd walk in with you," she said.

Dan usually preferred his own company on the walk to school, but he wasn't upset to see her. She had this knack of involving you in the conversation. They talked about *In Scene* – a TV music show they both liked – arguing about who was the best band. The walk went really quickly and put Dan in a slightly better mood.

In class, Miss Foxton asked who'd come up with ideas for their presentations. Most pupils put their hands up; Dan kept his hand firmly down, as did several others. A few people had already started working on their presentations. Someone was doing a radio show about the local football team; someone else was doing a slideshow about their recent trip to Italy.

During lunch, Dan was sitting with Lucy in the canteen, when three boys approached them. Lucy pulled a face. It was the class 'hard man', Steve Fenton with his sidekicks Tony Law and Gavin Reith. According to Lucy, Steve topped the category of 'avoid at all costs'.

Steve and his henchmen were dressed in identikit jeans, trainers and black jackets. Steve had a spotty face, a thin covering of hair above his top lip and dark brown eyes.

"School dinners aren't good enough for you?" asked Steve, leaning over them and staring at Dan's lunch box.

Steve's breath smelt of crisps.

"It's none of your business," replied Lucy.

"I don't eat meat," said Dan to Steve.

"You're a vegetarian?" asked Steve.

"Something like that. I don't eat bacon or pork and some other stuff," replied Dan.

Steve frowned. "Why not?" he demanded.

"Because I'm... Jewish."

Steve's eyes widened with surprise, but before he could get a word in, Lucy spoke.

"That's amazing!" she cried. "We had a Hindu girl once, but she only stayed a term. I've never met any Jewish people. Can you take me to a synagogue?"

"Shut it!" Steve hissed, glaring at her.

"Clear off, Steve," snapped Lucy, turning to face Dan. "We did it in Mr Casson's class last year," she said. "Muslims eat *halal* meat, Jews have *kosher*, so in terms of..."

"You hear that, lads?" said Steve, cutting Lucy off. "The guy's never eaten bacon."

Right on cue, Tony and Gavin started giggling.

"You're pathetic, Steve," said Lucy angrily.

"It's OK," said Dan, hoping to end this

particular exchange as quickly as possible.

"No, it's not OK," said Steve, taking a step forward. "You can't go your whole life without tasting bacon."

"It doesn't bother me," Dan replied.

Steve looked Dan up and down. "Come down the caff with us after school," he grinned. "I'll get you some bacon; my treat."

"No thanks," Dan replied, "I'm fine without it."

Steve shrugged his shoulders. "OK," he scowled, "whatever."

He swaggered away down the corridor with Tony and Gavin. He whispered something to them and they both burst out laughing and turned back to look at Dan.

Dan eyed Steve with uncertainty.

In London, being Jewish had never been an issue. There were quite a few other Jewish kids in his school and anyway, no one really cared about your religion or your background.

"Don't worry about Steve," said Lucy quietly. "He's all mouth."

"Yeah, I can see that," said Dan, turning to

his locker.

But in truth, this exchange had riled him a bit and he could feel an uncomfortable thread of anxiety twisting in the centre of his stomach.

WEDNESDAY

The name-calling started the following morning.

Miss Foxton's class were on their way to assembly, when Steve Fenton brushed past Dan and whispered something into his ear. He said it loud enough so that Dan would hear, but quiet enough so that no one else could.

"Bacon Boy."

Dan felt his cheeks redden. He stared at Steve who was now chatting and laughing at the front of the line with Tony and Gavin.

It's no big deal, Dan told himself. *Steve's just trying to wind me up. If he does it again, I'll just ignore him.*

But Steve did do it again; lots of times. Whenever he was near Dan he'd hiss the phrase in his ear.

Bacon Boy.

Bacon Boy.

Bacon Boy.

By lunchtime, Steve was beginning seriously to get on Dan's nerves, but Dan wasn't sure what to do. Should he tell someone – Miss Foxton, his parents, maybe Lucy? It was tempting but he didn't want to make a big deal about it. After all, a bit of name-calling wasn't the end of the world. No, he'd sit tight and not rise to the bait. Surely Steve would get bored of getting no reaction and go to bother someone else.

Straight after lunch, Miss Foxton wrote five names on the board.

Dan's was among them.

"OK," she said, "you five haven't chosen your presentation topic yet. Everyone else has chosen and most have begun putting their presentations together. So I'm setting you a deadline. You have until tomorrow morning to come up with an idea and to get cracking with it. If you don't, then I'll choose something for you."

Dan sighed heavily.

His brain was completely empty of presentation ideas. Lucy had suggested he do something about running, but if he couldn't be bothered to put on his tracksuit, he wasn't going to start making some multimedia show about the sport.

He'd checked his old piggy bank last night. All that was in there was a solitary ten pence coin and an IOU from Mum for five pounds. That wasn't exactly the budget for a grand escape, was it?

As he was getting his coat from the cloakroom after school, he felt a shove in his back.

"You taking your girlfriend anywhere special tonight, *Bacon Boy*?"

Dan swore under his breath. "She's not my girlfriend," he replied, glaring at Steve Fenton, who was hovering beside him with a smug grin.

"Whatever," sneered Steve, "but make sure you choose a place that has bacon on the menu."

Steve slunk off to join Tony and Gavin who were waiting for him and smirking.

On the walk home with Lucy, Dan tried to block out the image of Steve Fenton's face and the phrase he'd been taunting him with all day.

Lucy was already well on the way with her presentation. She was using her dad's camcorder to make a film about snakes. Her older brother had two pet ones and she'd spoken to someone at the zoo who said she could do some filming there.

As he listened to Lucy, Dan made himself a promise. *As soon as I get home, I'm going to give my presentation some serious thought. I don't want Miss Foxton choosing it for me.*

But when he got in, he had to watch a couple of his favourite TV shows, he sneaked a bit of supper from the kitchen and then there was a live football match on the radio. By the time his brain finally came to focus on his presentation, it was half past ten and he was exhausted.

OK, he promised himself. *I'll wake up early tomorrow morning and have a topic ready for Miss Foxton by the time I get to school.*

He set his alarm for seven a.m. and crashed out.

THURSDAY

As soon as Dan's alarm went off he reached for the snooze button and immediately fell back to sleep. He repeated this process three times and when he eventually did get up, he was too busy reading the football reports in the morning's papers, to give his presentation any thought.

Relax, I'll think of something on the way to school.

But he'd downloaded a great album on to the MP3 player he'd got for his last birthday, and the music was still going when he arrived at the school gates. He checked his watch. He was ten minutes early.

OK, I'll go to the toilet and by the time I've finished, I'll have a presentation topic all worked out.

He headed to the boys' toilets at the far side of the playground. A minute later, he was just washing his hands when the door flew open and in walked Steve, Tony and Gavin.

Dan's heart sank.

"Watcha *Bacon Boy*," grinned Steve.

Tony and Gavin laughed.

"What do you want?" asked Dan irritably.

"I've been talking to my uncle about you," said Steve. "He told me all this stuff about how powerful Jews are – says your lot are running the country."

Dan stared at Steve in shock. What was he on about? If Jews were running the country he would have got some of the really powerful ones to block his family's move up to Wareham and not end up facing an idiot like Steve Fenton!

Steve edged a step closer. Dan felt his palms going clammy. He looked round the toilet. If he tried to barge past Steve and his mates they'd easily stop him and probably batter him.

No, I'm going to tough this out.

He thought about his answer for a few seconds. "OK," said Dan, forcing his voice to remain calm. "If Jews are running the country, how come the Prime Minister isn't Jewish? Or the head of the army? Or those country squires who own all of the land?"

Steve was stumped for a moment and in the tense silence, the toilet door suddenly swung open and a small boy came running in with a desperate expression on his face.

"Get lost!" shouted Steve.

The boy stared in terror at Steve and ran back out.

"Don't try and twist the truth with words, *Bacon Boy,*" hissed Steve. "Maybe they *are* really Jews but they just hide it. My uncle knows what he's talking about. He's a local councillor."

Dan knew that several overtly racist councillors had been elected recently. He gulped nervously. This thing with Steve was beginning to turn ugly. But in spite of the unease and fear he felt rising and falling with every breath, he still was determined to deal with Steve by himself.

"Your uncle may be a councillor," said Dan quietly, "but that doesn't mean he knows what he's talking about."

"Are you calling my uncle a liar?" demanded

Steve, taking two paces towards Dan, his face now less than a ruler's length away from Dan's face.

"I don't know your uncle, but that stuff he's telling you is wrong."

"You better watch yourself, *Bacon Boy*," seethed Steve.

"Or what?" said Dan.

At that second the toilet door swung open again and Mr Fairbridge – one of Oakridge's toughest teachers - stomped in.

"Did one of you just tell Alfie Rodham he couldn't use these toilets?" he fumed.

"No," replied Steve, his face suddenly all angelic and innocent, "he must have got his wires crossed."

"Well what are you lot doing in here anyway?" demanded Mr Fairbridge.

"We're just leaving," said Dan, sidestepping Steve and his cronies and walking out. A second later the other three spilled into the pale morning light.

"I haven't finished with you, *Bacon Boy*," hissed Steve as he led the others up the playground.

"What was all that about?"

Dan spun round.

It was Lucy.

He felt his cheeks reddening. "Nothing," he said quickly.

"Really?" asked Lucy. "It didn't look like nothing."

"Yeah, forget about it," nodded Dan firmly.

"OK," Lucy said, after a brief silence, "let's go. Have you chosen a subject for your presentation?"

***

"Right, Dan," said Miss Foxton a few minutes later, "the other four have chosen their topic. Have you chosen yours?"

Dan was about to say no, but for some reason his mouth said, "*Yes.*"

He frowned at his answer.

"Good," smiled Miss Foxton. "Are you going to share it with us?"

"Erm… n… no, not yet," Dan heard his mouth stuttering. "What I mean is, I want to get started first and then I'll tell you."

Miss Foxton nodded encouragingly. "So long as

you get cracking on it this morning, that's fine."

"What is it?" whispered Lucy.

She was busily arranging the pieces for her snake film storyboard on the table.

Dan shrugged his shoulders. "I'm not sure," he whispered back.

Lucy looked confused. "What do you mean?" she demanded. "You just told Miss Foxton that you knew."

Dan pulled a face.

The truth was, he didn't know. His mouth seemed to have developed a life of its own. And then without any warning, his feet made him stand up and walk across the classroom. It felt unbelievably weird, like his body was deciding its own moves without him. Five seconds later, he found himself standing in front of the tall metal art cupboard.

What am I doing here? I'm rubbish at art.

But even as this thought was going through his brain, he felt his hands reaching out and opening the art cupboard doors. He stood for a minute, staring at the shelves, laden with different materials. There were beads, paint, scrap paper, felt tip pens, bags of assorted material and a large packet of art pencils. On the top shelf was a large brown paper package filled with clay.

Dan's hands reached out, prised open the package and broke off two huge chunks of clay.

What the hell is going on? The only thing I've ever made out of clay was supposed to be a spaceship but ended up looking like a broken pumpkin!

But this didn't halt the process at all. Immediately, he was marching back to his desk, with the two lumps of smooth, cool clay in his hands.

Lucy looked up and raised an eyebrow. "What's with the clay?" she asked. "Are you doing some sort of sculpture for your presentation?"

Dan dropped the clay chunks onto the desk. "Yeah... something like that... I think."

Lucy gave him a baffled look but returned to her storyboard.

Dan stood over the table trying to work out what was going on, but he didn't have to wait long. Suddenly, his hands broke the clay lumps into several smaller pieces and started rolling them into various shapes of different sizes. Once again, they seemed to be operating totally by themselves, without any instruction from him.

He stared down at the desk in amazement as his hands pulled and fashioned the smooth brown lumps. They worked at the clay for over an hour and before he knew it the lesson was over.

Dan was in a state of shock.

He'd created a series of clay shapes, some long and thin, others round. He had absolutely no idea what they represented or how his hands were going to fit them together, if indeed that was the plan. Lucy started packing up for the day and stared down at his 'work in progress'.

"That looks interesting," she remarked. "Are you going to tell me what it is yet?"

"You'll see when it's finished," Dan replied mysteriously.

And hopefully, so will I.

Dan wrapped up the clay pieces in some tissues from Miss Foxton's desk before carrying them back to the art cupboard and sealing them inside the paper package with the rest of the clay.

**

Lying in bed that night, Dan thought about his unpleasant meeting with Steve Fenton in the toilets. He shivered. Steve really gave him the creeps and this rubbish his uncle was telling him was dangerous stuff. Although he wished Steve would just give up with the whole Bacon Boy thing, something told him that wasn't going to happen.

Then his thoughts turned to the way his hands had worked on the clay so independently in class. What on earth was it they were making and why didn't he know? If he told Lucy about any of this, she'd probably think he was a complete fruitcake.

He sighed and turned out the light.

Hopefully I'll finish the model tomorrow. At least then the suspense will be over.

FRIDAY

Dan's hands worked on his clay model throughout Friday morning. He still had no idea what he was actually constructing, but as the morning progressed, he saw it beginning to take shape. It was a man of some sort. It looked a bit like a huge caveman. He watched as his fingers added two eyes, a nose and a mouth.

"That looks interesting," smiled Miss Foxton, leaning over the table and taking a look. "Is it finished?"

"Er... I... I... I think so," replied Dan.

"Great!" she nodded. "Tell you what; I'll give it to Miss Bolton and ask her to fire it in the school kiln before the end of the day. Then you can take it home tonight to begin the talking bit of your presentation."

Dan nodded. "OK... er... yeah."

True to her word, Miss Foxton returned the

model man to Dan at the end of the day. It had been fired and now looked shiny and realistic – a huge, slightly fierce-looking earth giant.

Dan felt very upbeat as he headed to his locker after school. He was delighted with the clay model he was carrying. OK, he didn't understand how his hands had made it of their own accord, but he felt there was definitely something special about it.

He pulled open his locker to get his rucksack and the smile immediately leapt off his face. There facing him on the locker shelf was his pencil case. In thick black letters, someone had scrawled the words *DIRTY JEW* across its surface.

Dan felt as if he'd just been punched in the stomach.

It was easy to break into people's lockers, it happened all the time. But to break in and do something like this was really disgusting. And it didn't take a rocket scientist to work out who was responsible for this hateful graffiti

He checked the corridor. There were lots of people around but no sign of Steve or his disciples. He turned back to his locker and held the pencil case in his hands.

"Hey Dan, what's up?"

It was Lucy.

Dan quickly shoved the case back into his locker. "I was just thinking about running," he lied.

"Are you going home now?" she asked.

"Er… no. I've got a couple of things to do. I'm in a bit of a hurry." He needed to be alone; to have some time to think.

"OK," nodded Lucy. "I'll see you tomorrow."

As he hurried home, Dan pondered the scorching questions burning in his mind. The Steve Fenton trouble was getting more serious by the minute; the name-calling; Steve's racist nonsense about Jews controlling the country; and now the anti-Semitic daubing on his pencil case. Was it time to tell Miss Foxton?

No, I can still handle this thing. It's early days. Maybe this pencil case scrawl will be the end of it — the final insult.

***

"What have you got there?" asked Mum, as Dan sat in his bedroom after supper, gazing at the model man on his desk.

"It's nothing," he replied, pushing it under a running magazine.

"Is it made of clay?"

Dan nodded.

Mum gave him a funny look. "You've never liked making things with clay."

"I know, it's just something Miss Foxton got us to do."

Mum smiled. "OK," she said, "but don't stay up too late reading that running magazine."

"I won't," he replied.

Mum shut the bedroom door behind her and Dan listened as her feet took her back downstairs. He pulled the model out and stood it on the desk in front of him.

Who are you, Mr Clay Warrior? And where do you come from?

At that moment Dan noticed that there was a strange orangey/yellow glow coming from the centre of the model man's chest. It was like a circle of pulsating fire. Dan stared at it in complete shock, but before he could do anything, he was suddenly surrounded by a searing flash of white light. It was so bright that he screwed up his eyes in pain. A split second later there was a popping sound and he felt the light fade.

***

Cautiously Dan opened his eyes. To his astonishment, he was no longer in his bedroom. Instead, he found himself standing on a narrow strip of sand, about twenty metres away from the edge of a river. He could feel an icy wind stabbing at his cheeks and tiny pebbles under his trainers.

He closed his eyes again.

This must be a dream. When I open my eyes I'll wake up and be back in my bedroom.

He opened his eyes again.

He was still by the river.

This wasn't a dream.

But if it wasn't a dream, how did he get here and where on earth was he?

Quickly, he checked the buildings on either side

of the river. They looked old – very old. He turned his attention back to the water. There were three silhouetted figures up ahead. They were standing a couple of metres into the river, knee deep in water.

Dan crept forward, until he got a clearer view of them.

It was three men. Two of them were young – in their mid-twenties, with short hair and earnest faces. The other man was much older. He had white hair and a white beard. The older man was calling out some sort of instructions to the younger men in a language Dan had never heard. The younger men responded to the older guy's shouts by wading deeper into the water.

Dan was completely fascinated. What were they doing? It wasn't exactly sunbathing weather. Their legs must be freezing.

He was about to take another couple of steps towards them, when there was another blinding flash of light and he found himself back in his bedroom.

As his eyes readjusted to the light, he looked around him.

There was no sign of the three men or of the sand or the river.

He stared at the model man on his desk. It had stopped glowing. What had he *created* here? The model seemed to have some sort of special powers. But this wasn't Indiana Jones and some ancient artefact. This was Wareham, not some kind of sci-fi movie.

He stared at the model for half an hour until finally tumbling into bed, exhausted.

But there were two things very clear in Dan's mind. He *had* left his bedroom. And he *had* been to that river and seen those men.

SATURDAY

"That clay model I made in school, is a bit freaky," said Dan to Lucy the next morning, as they sat on a bench in the local park.

"Freaky? In what way?"

Dan took a deep breath. He'd thought a lot about whether or not to tell Lucy about last night's extraordinary event, and finally decided he had to share it with her or else he'd go mad.

He described exactly what had happened.

Lucy listened carefully.

When Dan had finished, she didn't start laughing and telling him he was a head-case, as he'd expected.

"And the model only glowed for a few seconds?" she asked.

Dan nodded.

"You know what I think?" Lucy replied. "I think you were really, really tired, and you sort of half fell asleep at your desk. I've done it loads of times. You were half asleep and half awake and you had this weird dream about the model."

"It *wasn't* a dream," Dan replied.

"All right, it was more like a *day*dream."

"It wasn't *any* kind of dream," he said firmly. "I was wide awake – I'm telling you. I went to that river and saw those men."

Lucy sensed his irritation. "OK," she replied, "whatever."

***

An hour after Dan got back from the park, he was sitting up in his room, cradling the clay model.

"We're going out for a walk," called Mum up the stairs. "Why don't you come?"

"No thanks," Dan shouted back. There was no way he was leaving the house at the minute.

He gazed at the model on his desk.

Come on warrior man, give off that glow again. Take me back to that river.

A couple of hours later, the model hadn't given off even the tiniest of glows. Dan's parents weren't back yet. He walked over to his cupboard and slipped on his tracksuit. However much he hated Wareham and missed his mates back home, he'd decided to resume training. Running made him feel good, physically and mentally. It was time to get out there again. Maybe if he got back to his best form, he could persuade some company to sponsor his move back to London? It was a long shot, but you never knew.

He pushed the model man to the back of his bedroom cupboard and set out.

Dan jogged down his street, turned the corner, ran past the off-licence and cut over towards a bridge that stretched over the canal. His feet pounded over the bridge and he turned left, arriving on the canal towpath. A minute later, he'd hit his stride. It felt good to get some air into his lungs and feel the ground beneath his trainers.

He was running at a decent pace now, the air zipping past him. In the sky a weak ray of sun was trying to get past a blanket of grey clouds.

He passed a couple of colourfully-painted narrow boats and a dilapidated, lock keeper's cottage. He was just going past the back of an industrial estate, when a hand suddenly appeared from nowhere and grabbed him by the throat.

He was dragged sideways and then felt his back being slammed against a brick wall. He slumped to the floor and yelped in pain.

He looked up and his body shuddered.

It was Steve Fenton with Tony and Gavin.

The four of them were on a narrow pathway surrounded by a high fence that led towards the car park at the back of the industrial estate.

"This is our hang-out," said Steve. "Nice of you to pop in for a visit."

Dan stood up and rubbed his aching back. "I'm out of here," he said.

Tony and Gavin moved to block his escape.

Dan took a deep breath. "What do you want?" he asked.

"My uncle's been telling me loads more stuff about Jews," Steve hissed.

"Oh yeah?" Dan asked. "I suppose you're going to tell me all about it."

"Don't try and be clever, *Bacon Boy*," snapped

Steve. "I know all about you lot. I know how rich you all are and how you keep all your money to yourselves."

Dan couldn't stop himself laughing.

"What's so funny?" Steve growled, shoving Dan on the shoulder.

"Jews are all rich," snorted Dan. "You've got to be joking!"

"Do I look like I'm joking?" sneered Steve.

"It's just that... well... unfortunately, my family doesn't really fit in with that theory."

"Oh yeah?" challenged Steve. "Why is that?"

"Er... we aren't exactly what you'd call *rich*," Dan replied. "In fact the reason we moved up here was so that my parents could try and pay off their debts. They borrowed loads of money to buy our house in London and they couldn't keep up with the payments. They owe the bank thousands and thousands of pounds. So my mum got a promotion, they sold the house, we moved up here and we bought a much smaller house. Does that sound like we're rich?"

Steve's mouth hung open for a few seconds,

like a bewildered dog.

"You're lying," he eventually hissed.

"I'm not," Dan replied. "Come round and look at my parents' credit card bills and bank letters."

Steve turned to Tony and Gavin. They looked back at him with blank expressions.

"Look, Steve," Dan said quietly, "if Jews are so rich, my family would be living in a far bigger house than yours, wouldn't they?"

Steve scowled.

"I've seen *your* house," Dan continued. "It's much bigger than mine; you've got a much flasher car and you've got satellite TV. We've got a beaten-up banger and only five TV channels. You can't tell me that makes us rich."

"Well… maybe you're not, but the rest of them are."

"That's rubbish," Dan replied. "There are loads of Jewish people living below the breadline."

This information was clearly too much for Steve because he suddenly lashed out and kicked Dan in the stomach. Dan doubled over in pain and fell to the floor. He gasped for breath.

Steve kicked him again, this time on the leg.

Dan winced.

Steve stood over him.

"You're just being clever with words," Steve yelled. "My uncle says you're all rich, so you're all rich."

Dan's fists were clenched in fury. He'd love to stand up and charge at Steve, but Tony and Gavin were part of the equation. If he did lunge for their leader, they'd mash him.

It looked like Steve was going to kick him again, but the sound of a siren sounded nearby.

Steve glared at Dan, looked at his henchmen and then the three of them legged it. A couple of minutes later, Dan emerged back onto the towpath. The sound of the siren had died down and the only people he could see were two old guys with fishing rods, about fifty metres down on the other side of the water.

Dan's stomach and legs ached. He limped home and ran a hot bath to ease the bruises donated to him by Steve.

***

"There's a great film on TV tonight," said his mum later on, as afternoon slipped into evening. "We could all watch it together. I've got some pizzas in the freezer."

Dan shook his head. "I've got homework."

Mum looked at him with shock. "Homework?" she enquired. "Since when did homework take precedence over pizza and a movie?"

Dan shrugged and headed up to his room. He shut the door and reached for the model in the back of his cupboard. He placed it on his desk and sat down in front of it.

He sat there the whole way through the film his parents were watching downstairs. He sat there well after they called out 'goodnight'. He sat there past midnight.

But the model didn't glow.

Dan felt his eyes closing and his head drooping on to his desk.

When he woke up, his mouth felt as if it was full of cotton wool.

He checked his watch. The digits blinked back at him. 2.07 a.m.

The clay model was there on his desk and this time its chest *was* glowing.

Dan sat bolt upright as a searing flash white light engulfed him.

A second later, he found himself back by the river.

Lucy had been wrong.

This wasn't a dream.

He really *was* here.

The three men were exactly where he'd seen them last time, except now he was only ten metres away from them. The older guy was shouting out more instructions in the foreign language at the two younger men, but now he was gesticulating wildly with his arms. Dan took a couple of steps forward. The younger guys were scooping great handfuls of mud out of the river and placing them on the sand. They'd already accumulated several massive piles of the stuff.

A few moments later, they stopped collecting the mud and started pummelling and rolling it with their palms and fists.

They're making something.

As they fashioned the mud, the older man grew more and more animated.

Ten minutes later, a chill of terror snaked down Dan's spine, as he realised what they were making.

It was an enormous mud man – an exact replica of the clay model he'd made in school!

Dan shivered in disbelief.

This was getting *seriously* weird.

A couple of minutes later, they'd carved eyes, a nose and a mouth on to the mud man's oversized head. Then the two young men pulled the mud man up to a standing position.

It was huge – well over eight feet tall.

Dan stared in astonishment as the men held it steady. The giant mud man towered over its creators. They stood rooted to the spot, gazing up at it in awe.

Suddenly the old man began to circle the mud man, reciting some sort of chant. The mud man stood on the sand – a huge, lifeless statue.

The old man reached up to touch the mud man's face and then placed something inside its mouth. As soon as he'd done this, the mud man suddenly began to stretch its arms and legs.

Dan's eyes nearly popped out of their sockets.

The statue was alive!

But that's impossible! It's made of mud! I saw it being built!

The mud man twisted its shoulders and swivelled its head. Its gaze fell upon Dan.

Dan gulped nervously and took a few steps backwards.

The three men turned and stared at Dan with anxious, suspicious frowns. A second later, the mud man pushed its right foot forward and began marching menacingly towards him.

Dan's heart froze

One of the younger men shouted something.

For Dan, there was only one option.

He turned and fled.

His heart beat wildly as the blood pounded a frantic rhythm between his ears. He could hear the huge footsteps of the mud man crashing behind him and its rasping, noisy breath. Dan sped past a wooden sign stuck on to a stone wall and then through a small clump of wiry trees. He glanced over his shoulder and saw to his horror that the mud man was nearly upon him. It was stretching out its two giant mud hands to grab him.

Dan's whole body shook with terror. His left foot suddenly crashed against a boulder on the sand. He lost his balance and spiralled forward onto the ground.

The enormous shadow of the mud man loomed over him. Its left hand grabbed Dan by the scruff of the neck as its chest glowed a bright orangey/yellow.

The terrifying creature then raised its right hand.

Dan felt as if his life was about to be terminated.

He closed his eyes and screamed.

SUNDAY

"Lucy?"

There was silence for a few seconds.

"Who is this?" Lucy croaked.

"It's Dan."

There was another silence.

"Dan? It's seven a.m. on SUNDAY morning. Call me later."

"This can't wait," Dan replied urgently. "I need you to come round to my house now, before my parents get up."

"This is a joke, right?"

"No Lucy. It's deadly serious."

Lucy muttered irritably. "OK," she said, "I'm on my way."

Ten minutes later Dan was leading Lucy up into the loft with a finger over his lips.

The Bernsteins' loft was rectangular, with a low

sloping ceiling. There were cardboard packing boxes strewn across the floor.

"This had better be good," Lucy hissed.

Dan stepped past a large pile of yellowing newspapers and several old tins of paint, left there by the previous owners. At the far side of the room was a tall brown cupboard.

"Well go on," said Lucy, rubbing the sleep out of her eyes, "what is it?"

Dan called softly in the direction of the cupboard. "You come out now?"

"It's a cupboard," Lucy groaned. "You've got me out of bed to show me your conversation with a cupboard. That's so... "

But before she finished her sentence, a large brown leg eased out from behind the cupboard, followed by another leg, two arms, a body and a head.

Lucy held her hand over her mouth.

"*Oh,*" she whispered, staring up at this huge statue of a man. "It's... it's... just like the model you made in school. Where on earth did you get enough clay for *this* one? You must have used buckets of the stuff."

"I didn't make this one," Dan said.

"I don't get it. Was it already here?"

Dan looked up at the mud man's eyes. "Turn round," he said.

The mud man turned through three hundred and sixty degrees.

"Excellent!" mouthed Lucy. "Where are the controls? Let me have a go!"

"It doesn't have controls," Dan whispered.

"It must have controls!" she insisted. "Come on Dan, don't mess me about."

Lucy strode forward and began to examine the mud body for signs of a battery compartment or wires.

There were none.

She stared from Dan to the mud giant and back to Dan again.

"Well, where did you find him?" she demanded.

"It's connected to that freaky thing I told you about," Dan replied softly.

Lucy's mouth opened in amazement. "What? The glowing model transporting you to the river?"

"Yes," Dan replied. "I went there again only this time I brought someone back with me."

Lucy's mouth opened even wider.

"The two younger guys were making him from river mud," Dan explained. "The old man put something in his mouth and he suddenly came to life. He started stomping after me. I thought he was going to kill me. But when the white light flashed again, I ended up back in my bedroom, with him!"

"And he doesn't want to kill you?" asked Lucy.

Dan shook his head. "He's done everything I've asked him so far, which has mainly been coming up here with me and hiding. I can't let my parents find out about this. They'd probably just go to the police or something."

"Is that such a bad thing?" asked Lucy.

"I…I…think he's here for a reason. I don't know what it is, but I'm going to find out. And if the police take him away, I won't be able to do that."

"So what are we going to do?"

Dan smiled. Lucy had said *we*. She wanted to be involved. He was so relieved to have someone else on board.

Lucy bit her bottom lip. "Look Dan," she started, "I'm really sorry I didn't believe you the other day."

"It doesn't matter," Dan replied. "I just needed you to come over and see him. I thought I was going mad."

Lucy pulled her ponytail tighter in her hairband. "Did you get any clues about where you were?"

Dan scratched his cheek. "Just before I ran away, one of the young guys shouted out something. It sounded like 'Leeb' or 'Lobe,' or something like that."

"Was there anything else?"

Dan nodded. "I passed a wooden sign with some numbers on."

"What were they?"

"There was a 1 and a 5, but I don't remember the others."

"Have you tried the Internet?"

"Of course; I've been through five search engines, trying all the spellings of both words by themselves, and then in combination with 1 and 5."

"Anything?"

"Nothing."

"And you've no idea *where* this river was?"

"No idea at all. But it was definitely a long time ago."

"So what next?" asked Lucy.

"If the Internet can't help us," Dan mused, "I reckon we should try the library in town."

"But it's Sunday," Lucy pointed out.

"It's open on Sundays this month – to see if people use it," Dan replied. "I saw a notice."

"Right," nodded Lucy briskly, "I'm going home to get my stuff. Call for me in an hour."

Before leaving the house, Dan visited the loft five times. By now his parents were up and about.

"What are you doing up there?" Mum asked.

Dan felt his cheeks going red. "There's just some interesting old stuff up there – postcards, letters, things like that."

"Really?" asked Dad. "Maybe I'll come up and join you."

"No," snapped Dan a bit too firmly.

His dad eyed him quizzically.

"I'm… I'm… just… enjoying looking through it alone," Dan replied.

"OK," replied Dad. "I'll leave it to you."

***

The town centre library was arranged on three floors – each one looking exactly the same. A long wooden lending desk stretched along the left hand wall; a series of desks were set out in rows in the centre of the room; two of the remaining walls were covered in bookshelves, while the other wall was home to ten computers with broadband Internet access.

Dan and Lucy were sitting at desks, encyclopaedias and reference books piled high in front of them. It was midday. They'd been here for three hours, only breaking once to buy some crisps and cans of drink from the vending machine on the ground floor.

Their research so far had been fruitless.

"This is never going to happen," said Lucy.

"OK," Dan sighed, feeling sure Lucy was right. "Let's give it ten more minutes and then get out of here."

Lucy nodded and returned to a huge reference book.

Dan stood up and went for a wander.

He strolled past the towering shelves, running his left thumb over hundreds of book spines, as if doing this might somehow pass on some vital clue to him. But nothing leapt forward to point him in the right direction.

We've done our best, but we've failed. LEEB or LOBE or whatever it was, and 15, will have to remain a mystery.

He was just beginning to feel the disappointment really sinking in when his gaze was diverted towards a set of very thick textbooks someone had left on a desk. He ambled over and looked at their covers.

Key Dates in Muslim History; Key Dates in Jewish History; Key Dates in Christian History.

Out of interest, he flicked the Jewish book open and thumbed through the first few pages. It was all about tribes wandering through hot, dusty deserts.

Reams and reams of dates and events were splattered all over the pages and Dan sighed deeply with frustration.

He was just about to close the book and get Lucy, when a number leaped out of the page at him.

1580.

It felt like a dial had just been twisted in his brain.

That was it! That was the number he'd seen on the wooden sign!

He dragged his index finger quickly down the page, taking in events that had happened in 1580, in places as far apart as Jerusalem and Rome and Syria.

And then he saw it.

1580. PRAGUE. CZECHOSLOVAKIA. RABBI LOEB.

He mouthed the name under his breath.

LOEB. Could that be the word the young guy had shouted?

He quickly scanned the entry and his heartbeat increased with every word he read. He snatched up the book and rushed back to Lucy, nearly knocking over a young librarian staggering under the weight of a pile of books.

"I think I've got it," he hissed in Lucy's ear.

Her eyes lit up immediately.

He dropped the book down on the desk and pointed to the entry.

They immediately started reading in silence.

The Legend of the Golem of Prague

In 1580, attacks on Jews in the Czechoslovakian capital city, Prague, were escalating at an alarming rate. The entire Jewish community felt under threat. Legendary community leader, Rabbi Loeb, decided to create a 'Golem' (pronounced Go-lem) – a creature steeped in kaballah (Jewish mysticism). The sole purpose of the Golem was to defend the Jewish community and to attack those who sought to destroy it. Using two young disciples as his workmen, Rabbi Loeb oversaw the creation of the Golem from Danube river mud. When the

Golem was completed, Rabbi Loeb chanted mystical incantations and gave the Golem life, by placing a piece of parchment with Hebrew writing inside its mouth. Following the Golem's creation, attacks on the Jewish community in Prague declined noticeably, while several anti-Jewish rabble-rousers were hurt or killed in mysterious circumstances.

"He's the Golem of Prague!" hissed Dan. "He must be!"

"But why is he here?" whispered Lucy. It must be something to do with you being Jewish!"

Thoughts of Steve Fenton, his anti-Jewish rants and the *DIRTY JEW* scrawl on his pencil case flew through Dan's mind. Could the Golem be somehow connected to Steve Fenton? Should he tell Lucy about the Steve 'situation'? He was tempted but was sure she'd freak out and demand to get Miss Foxton involved. Dan didn't want that to happen – for now at least.

"I don't know," Dan replied. "This is 21st Century England, not 16th Century

Czechoslovakia, and besides, my family aren't being attacked."

"But what if he's here for some other Jewish people – ones facing danger? Maybe the Golem will go after their enemies," said Lucy.

"I don't think he'll do anything like that," replied Dan, deep in thought. "Like I said before, he's done everything I've told him. He hasn't been at all violent or anything."

"OK," replied Lucy, "but I think we should go straight back to yours now and plan what to do with him."

"Definitely," agreed Dan.

There were no buses so they ran all the way back to Dan's house. They burst through the front door and ran straight past Dan's mum who was standing in the hallway, talking on the phone.

"Hey you two, what's up?" she called as they sped upstairs.

They ignored the question and pelted straight up to the loft.

Dan strode over to the cupboard and peered behind it.

His face suddenly went white.

"What is it?" hissed Lucy urgently.

She hurried over and looked behind the cupboard. She immediately saw what was wrong. There was nothing there.

The Golem had vanished.

***

"Dan?" It was eleven p.m. when Lucy's mobile finally rang.

"He's back."

It had been an agonising day of searching. They had looked all over town, but there had been no sign of the Golem anywhere.

"Thank goodness for that. When did he make it?"

"About two minutes ago. He climbed in through the skylight window. He must have gone out that way."

"Has he talked yet?"

"No, he just came in and went straight behind the cupboard."

"He was out for hours. Where did he go?

This is crazy, Dan. Maybe we *should* tell someone about it?"

"No way!" snapped Dan. "We sit tight and try to figure out what's going on. As soon as we involve any grown-ups, they'll ruin everything."

"Maybe you're right," Lucy conceded with a yawn. "Let's talk about it in the morning."

MONDAY

Dan got up at five a.m., went up to the loft and called for the Golem to follow him. He led the mud man downstairs and out of the back door. Behind the Bernsteins' tiny garden was a service road that ran along the backs of all the houses on their side of the street. There were several dilapidated but just about usable garages out there and one came with the Bernsteins' new house. Dan and his dad had checked their garage out on the first day up here. It was full of cobwebs and grime, and damp, but Dan reasoned it would be a far safer place to hide the Golem – his parents were very unlikely to come out here.

Dan and Lucy spent most of the day holding whispered conversations about the Golem.

"What happens if he goes out again?" Lucy asked.

"I've told him not to and he's shown no signs of heading off again."

Lucy took a deep breath. "But what about all that stuff about him attacking people and those deaths in mysterious circumstances."

"I'm sure he's not going to kill anyone," Dan replied. "We've just got to be patient. I'm sure we're soon going to find out why he's here."

Lucy sighed wearily. "OK," she agreed, "but we can't keep it a secret for ever."

That evening, Dan told his parents he was going for a long run. He slipped into the service road behind the house and hurried into the garage. The Golem was sitting on a clump of empty packing crates – exactly as Dan had left him the night before.

"Are you OK?" Dan asked softly. "Is there anything I can get you?"

The Golem turned his head a fraction to look at Dan.

He said nothing.

Later that night, Dan paced his room, deep in thought. He really didn't want to tell anyone about the Golem, but what if Lucy was right? What would happen if he went out and attacked someone? There would be pandemonium. They'd probably call in the army and have tanks blasting missiles at the mud man. And if this happened, would the Golem be killed or injured? Maybe he was immune to pain? Dan could see the whole situation spinning out of control.

And if the Golem was connected to Steve Fenton, what was the giant man going to do? Was he going to hurt or even kill Steve? Dan disliked Steve intensely but he didn't want him to be *killed*.

He looked out of his window at the dark, damp street, illuminated by a line of street lamps. He made up his mind. He was going to keep this thing secret for a few more days – he had to give himself the chance to work out why the Golem was here. If things did start to go wrong, then he'd tell his parents or Miss Foxton.

TUESDAY

It was morning break and Dan was in the corridor putting his model Golem into his locker. He'd decided to keep it at school. At home, even if he carried on hiding it, his parents might discover it and start asking loads of questions. Dan was so wrapped up in his thoughts, that he didn't notice Steve Fenton and crew approaching.

"What's that?" asked Steve.

"Nothing," replied Dan, quickly shoving it inside his locker and turning the key.

"Don't think I've forgotten about you," snarled Steve.

Dan said nothing.

"I'm working on a little plan."

Dan frowned. He didn't like the sound of this. "What kind of plan?" he asked warily.

Steve tapped the side of his nose. "You'll see," he grinned, "don't you worry."

He swaggered off with Tony and Gavin close behind.

Later on in the day when Dan and Lucy were halfway home after school, they were, unsurprisingly, still talking about the mud man.

"I've been thinking about it all day," Lucy whispered, "and I really think we should tell someone."

"No!" insisted Dan, "I told you. We have to give ourselves some time to figure things out."

Lucy shook her head. "Come on, Dan. This could turn into something very dangerous. The Golem's caught up in all sorts of things – magic and time travel – stuff that is way beyond us."

"I know that," Dan replied testily, "but we need a chance."

"We have no idea what we're doing," Lucy insisted. "Please, Dan. Let's tell someone!"

It was at this point that Dan snapped. "DON'T TELL ME WHAT TO DO!" he shouted. "I discovered him and I'm the one who is going to decide what to do with him!"

"FINE!" shouted Lucy, tears welling up in her

eyes. "But don't come crawling back to me when he kills someone!"

"I WON'T!" yelled Dan.

Lucy turned round and stomped off down the street, her body heaving with sobs. Dan gritted his teeth. Half of him wanted to go after her and apologise but the other half was furious. He just hoped she wouldn't go blabbing to anyone, while he tried to crack the mystery.

***

"I'm going out for a run," Dan called out to his parents an hour after supper.

"Don't go too far," Mum replied, "it's a school night."

"OK," Dan agreed.

A minute later, he was back in the garage.

The Golem was sitting on his crate. "I'm glad you're here," he said.

Dan stared at him in shock. "You can speak?" he mouthed.

"Sit down," said the Golem. "We need to talk."

The Golem's voice was deep and clear.

Dan sat on another crate and they faced each other.

"The model you made in school," the Golem began, "that's what initially summoned me here. I knew you were in some sort of trouble."

"You mean the Steve Fenton thing?" Dan asked.

The Golem nodded solemnly. "Word got to me that he's crossed the line."

"Are you going to kill him?"

The Golem shook his head. "No," he replied, "I'm not going to kill him. Steve Fenton is ignorant and unpleasant. The other night when I disappeared, I went to check out his house. He happened to be talking to that uncle of his and I listened in to their conversation. What his uncle was spouting is deeply dangerous, but I have my eye on the situation. There is nothing imminent planned that would cause you serious pain or injury. And so far, you have dealt with him very well."

Dan felt a surge of pride in his chest. Coming from the Golem of Prague this was praise indeed.

"So... so... why are you still here," Dan asked.

The Golem stood up. The top of his head brushed against the garage ceiling.

"I need *you* to help *me*," whispered the Golem.

"*Me?*" gasped Dan. "What can *I* do?"

At that moment the Golem's chest started to glow with the orangey/yellow pulse. A second later, a flash of white surrounded them. The light then vanished as quickly as it appeared.

Dan and the Golem found themselves crouching behind a stone wall that flanked a graveyard in front of an old church. Long strips of grass poked out between the gravestones. The sun was sending rays of heat and light on to the ground; the sky was blue and cloudless.

Amongst the gravestones Dan spotted four boys. They were all about his age. The first boy had a white shirt, a brown waistcoat and black trousers. He was wearing a cap and his long hair rested in wisps in front of each ear. The others wore shorts and beige shirts. Each of them had close-cropped hair.

The boy with the hat was tied up with ropes against a gravestone and the others had placed a cardboard sign round his neck. There was some writing on the sign, but Dan couldn't read it. The three boys were shouting something at the fourth boy in a foreign language. The fourth boy was shouting back at them, his eyes wide with fear.

"What are they saying to him?" whispered Dan.

"They're saying that the Jews killed Jesus and that this Jewish boy must pay for that crime."

"Are you serious?" gasped Dan. "That's ridiculous!"

The Golem nodded sadly. "Of course it's ridiculous, but Jews have been attacked over this accusation for two thousand years."

"But Jesus was a Jew, right?"

"Yes," nodded the Golem. "That's what the Jewish boy is telling them. He's asking them why would Jews kill one of their own people. He's saying it was the Romans who killed Jesus."

"But they don't believe him, do they?"

"No," said the Golem. "In the 21st century, most serious Christian scholars acknowledge this is all true. Jesus was a Jew and the Romans crucified him. But this is not the 21st century, Dan. In these dangerous times, this idea about his death is commonly accepted to be true. The scene you are witnessing in this graveyard, is actually taking place over two hundred years before you were born."

Dan opened his mouth to reply but the shock stopped any words tumbling out.

At that second, the three boys took a few steps back and reached down on to the ground. Each of them picked up a handful of stones. Immediately one of them threw a stone towards the tied-up boy.

It missed him.

Then another boy threw a larger stone. It hit the Jewish boy on the side of the head and cut deep into his flesh. He gulped in pain as a trickle of blood seeped down his cheek.

Dan's attention was snatched away for a second by a movement to his right. He swung round and stared, but there was nothing there. It must have been a dog or another animal, he decided.

Quickly, he turned back to the graveyard scene and felt a wave of fury fizzing through his body.

What these three boys were doing to the Jewish boy was cruel and dangerous. Sure, they might not really understand what they were saying, but it didn't take a rocket scientist to figure out that throwing stones at a boy's head might cause him some very serious damage.

"What are you going to do?" asked Dan urgently, as he watched another stone slash the boy's cheek and open another wound.

The Golem picked up two large stones.

"*I'm* not going to do anything," said the Golem. "You are."

He handed the stones to Dan.

Dan immediately understood.

He took the stones from the Golem's outstretched hands and scrambled over the church wall. He leapt over a couple of gravestones and, keeping his body low, sprinted down a narrow stretch of grass between two rows of graves. As he neared the boys, he stood up, raised his arms high into the air and threw one of his stones.

It hit one of the attackers on the back. He shouted out in pain and spun round. The other assailants wheeled round too, as did the boy they were attacking. They all eyed him with astonishment.

My clothes must be freaking them out, thought Dan.

He took advantage of their surprise, to launch his second stone. It hit one of the attacker boys on the legs. Before the three could respond, Dan bent down and scooped up a handful of stones.

He sprinted on towards them.

"STAY AWAY FROM HIM!" shouted Dan with anger burning in his eyes.

The three attackers stared in terror at this figure flying towards them. In an instant they turned and fled, hurtling across the graveyard, leaping over graves and vanishing through a wooden gate at the far side.

Dan untied the Jewish boy and smiled at him.

The boy looked white with shock and for a minute Dan thought he was going to faint. But he stayed on his feet and Dan quickly led him out of the graveyard to where the Golem was waiting.

The Golem knelt down and spoke to the boy in his own language. The boy replied in fast, nervous sentences. The Golem patted him on the back and wiped some of the blood off the boy's face with his huge fingers.

"He lives this way," said the Golem, pointing rightwards down a rutted track. "About a mile away."

They tramped for ten minutes in silence. Dan was shaking with anger and shock, but was incredibly relieved that he'd been able to save the boy from serious injury. Two large blue bruises had appeared on the boy's head.

The boy stopped for a second and pointed over a large gate towards a small gathering of dwellings across a large field.

The Golem spoke to him again and shook his hand. The boy grabbed Dan's right hand and shook it as well, giving him a toothy grin. Dan smiled back and in a second, the boy was through the gate and pelting at full speed towards his home.

At that moment, the Golem's chest glowed. A flash of light surrounded them and a second later, they were back in Dan's garage.

WEDNESDAY

Dan was desperate to tell Lucy about his adventure the next day in school but he was still furious with her. Why had she been so insistent on telling grown-ups? Why couldn't she just trust him for a few days and see what happened?

And anyway, if he did tell Lucy about the graveyard, she'd definitely go blabbing to someone – if she hadn't already.

His eyes met hers only once the next day at school, but they both looked away instantly. It was clear that neither of them were in the mood to apologise.

During lunch break, Steve Fenton barged into Dan in the corridor but that was it for the day. Maybe the Golem's presence was in some way repelling Steve?

It was a very reassuring thought.

Dan's mind was elsewhere during supper that

night. He couldn't wait to go and see the Golem in the garage. Maybe they'd be going on another mission tonight?

"You're miles away, aren't you?" smiled his mum.

"What?" mumbled Dan. "Oh… yeah… I'm just thinking about running."

His parents exchanged a nod of satisfaction.

"It's good to see you getting back into it."

Dan gave a half-nod.

The Golem's chest began to glow as soon as Dan entered the garage. The light flashed and they ended up standing behind a clump of willow trees, on one side of a wide street. The street lamps were lit and there was a faint mist in the air. Ten metres to their left stood a large red brick building. Swinging creakily above the building's front door was a large metal sign, displaying a pewter tankard. Dotted along the road in both directions were several very old-fashioned cars, the kind Dan had seen in black-and-white movies.

"OK," whispered the Golem, fixing his eyes on Dan. "I want you to go inside. They have a speaker on in the cellar tonight."

"What kind of speaker?" asked Dan nervously.

"Doesn't matter," said the Golem. "Go in, find out how many people are in there and check out the atmosphere."

"Aren't you coming?" asked Dan.

"I think I might stick out a bit, don't you?" replied the Golem with a ghost of a smile on his face.

Dan shivered. "But you'll still be here when I come out?"

The Golem nodded solemnly. "Get in and get out as fast as you can," he said. "Our timing will be crucial."

"What shall I do if someone talks to me?"

"Keep your head down and say nothing."

Dan pulled his jacket collar tighter and walked towards the door. He glanced back once but the Golem was already out of sight.

The door opened on to a dimly-lit, narrow passageway that led to a flight of stone steps. Dan could hear muffled noises of what sounded like clapping and cheering.

At the bottom of the stairs was a wooden door

with a large panel of frosted glass in its centre. Dan quickly pushed it open and went through.

He found himself standing at the back of a low rectangular room, about the size of his classroom. The place was absolutely packed and he was faced with the backs of what looked like at least two hundred people.

The first thing to hit him was the heat. It was boiling in there. This sensation was closely followed by the reek of cigarette smoke and beer that wafted into his nostrils.

The people in front of Dan were all looking towards a stage at the far side of the room. The 'speaker' was obviously in mid-flow, because Dan could hear his booming voice, which every few seconds rose to a kind of shriek that sent the audience wild with excitement. They clapped and cheered and stamped their feet.

Dan stood on tiptoes to try and get a glimpse of the speaker, but all he could see over the ranks of the spectators, were the speaker's arms. They were inside the sleeves of a brown tweed jacket. Every so often the speaker raised them above his head and waved them around dramatically. Dan studied the faces of the people standing just in front of him. Their expressions veered from rapture to fury to excitement. The speaker seemed to be manipulating them at will.

The atmosphere in the room crackled with electricity. It felt sinister and dangerous. Dan remembered the Golem's instructions.

Get in and get out as fast as you can.

Two minutes later, he was back at the Golem's side behind the trees. He reported all that he had seen. The Golem pulled a grim face.

"Follow me," he whispered.

Keeping to the shadows they ran down the street, turned left and then stopped outside a high wire fence at the front of two large, grey buildings. The Golem produced several plastic packets of what looked like large, oblong, red sweets and placed them in Dan's hands.

"What are they?" asked Dan.

"Open them," ordered the Golem.

Dan quickly pulled them open.

The 'sweets' were actually slices of meat.

They smelled pretty bad.

"Dog treats," whispered the Golem.

Dan looked at the Golem in bewilderment. *"Dog treats?"*

"Throw one over the fence into that doorway," commanded the Golem.

Dan quickly launched one of the red bits high over the fence. It skidded along the ground into the doorway.

Ten seconds later, there was an outbreak of growling and barking from inside the buildings.

"It's a home for neglected dogs," explained the Golem, "but they don't feed them too well in there."

A spark of realisation leapt through Dan's brain. "We're going to…?

The Golem nodded. "When I say go, I want you to run back to that tavern at full speed, dropping pieces of meat as you go. I'll give you a good head start and then I'll let the dogs out. Keep going all the way down to that cellar and throw the meat inside."

Dan swallowed nervously. "What happens if

I don't make it? The dogs could attack me, couldn't they?"

The Golem grabbed him by the shoulders. "You will make it," he replied, "I'm counting on you."

And with that the Golem began to scale the fence. He reached the top and looked down at Dan. The Golem dropped down from the fence and stepped across the shadows into the doorway.

"NOW!" he hissed.

Dan ran like he'd never run before, dropping meat pieces every twenty metres or so. He could hear increasingly loud barking noises coming from the dogs' home. As he rounded the corner, he quickly glanced round.

A huge pack of dogs of all shapes and sizes was flying after him. Some were stopping to grab the dropped meat treats, others were just running as fast as they could after the distributor of these delights.

Dan's heart hammered against his ribcage.

He pounded forward, the tavern now only about fifty metres away. The yapping and roaring of the dogs was getting louder and louder and he stole another glance back. They were rapidly gaining on him. They looked like they'd eat anything – especially a juicy human holding some of their precious meat feasts.

Come on, come on, I'm nearly there.

Dan flew past the tavern's front door and took the steps three at a time.

The pack were so close on his heels, he could smell their saliva and dirty coats, right behind him. Their paws clattered on the stairs, their barks now completely wild. The meat trail was driving them crazy. Dan leapt down the last five steps, flung the door open and threw the remaining pieces of meat high into the air.

He held the door open as the gang of ravished dogs burst into the cellar.

What followed was absolute pandemonium.

The dogs didn't care about the lack of legroom. They wanted their meat and nothing would stand in their way.

The spectators screamed and cried out as the dogs plunged into their midst. Glasses of beer flew through the air, picture frames crashed off the walls, people screamed and toppled over. Dan watched in disbelief as the humans and animals were tangled up in a terrifying twist.

Finally, someone managed to push open a door at the far left hand side of the room, and the shrieking adults stamped into the cold night air, bruised and battered.

The dogs leapt on to every piece of meat they could, fighting each other for the spoils, yapping and yowling manically. They made quick work of the remaining meat, but it was nowhere near enough to satisfy their hunger. Now the meat was gone, they were scouring every surface to see if there was any more.

And then suddenly they began running straight towards Dan. In terror he looked down at his hands and saw the red stains on his palms and fingers. The dogs were after him, they'd kill him to get to that smell. In desperation, Dan held his hands up to his face for protection and in doing this felt something sticky on his jacket.

It was a lone piece of meat.

He grabbed it quickly and threw it as hard as

he could through the open door. A nanosecond later, the dogs turned and started speeding towards the exit. Dan leapt after them and when they'd gone out, fighting and bawling over the last meat fragment, he slammed the door shut.

He breathed an enormous sigh of relief and heard someone pulling open the door by the stairs. He turned but didn't see who it was; he just saw the door swinging shut behind them.

The barman eyed him suspiciously, but Dan took no notice. He hurried over to the men's toilets and went in.

Once inside the toilet, Dan grabbed a piece of rough soap and began scrubbing his hands furiously. He was halfway through, when he heard a chain flushing behind him and someone coming out of one of the cubicles.

Dan spun round and immediately saw the brown tweed jacket he'd spied on the stage. It was the speaker!

Dan looked up and as he took in the man's features, his heart felt like it had just been speared. He felt his throat constrict and his breathing become laboured.

The man looked at him angrily, grabbed him by the arm and started shouting something at him.

With revulsion and sheer terror, Dan knocked the man's arm away and shoved him backwards. The man staggered back against the wall and this gave Dan the vital few seconds he needed to get away.

Back in the cellar, the barman was moving around picking up shards of broken glass. Dan fled through the door at the back and up the stone steps. He was outside and back behind the trees in less than thirty seconds.

But where was the Golem?

He started to run in the direction of the dogs' home when he suddenly felt a firm hand on his shoulder.

Please don't let it be the speaker from the cellar! Please not him!

He turned and came face-to-face with the Golem. The Golem's chest was glowing.

***

It took Dan over an hour to stop shaking.

"I can't believe what just happened," he mouthed with horror.

"It's over," said the Golem, placing a firm and steadying hand on his shoulder, "we're back in your garage. We're safe."

"But the speaker!" whispered Dan. "It was…"

"I know," replied the Golem.

When Dan had calmed down, he fixed his eyes on the Golem.

"You know tonight," he started, "the place, the people, the whole thing… can… you actually *change* history?"

"I can make life hard for those with hatred in their hearts," replied the Golem. "And I can save the lives of individuals or small groups of people. That is why I travel through time - doing whatever I can."

A look of sadness suddenly came over the Golem's face.

"However," he went on, "I have no power to stop big historical events from taking place. These are set in stone and cannot be altered."

They were silent for a while and then Dan spoke. "But we did OK out there, didn't we?" he said.

The Golem nodded, his expression brightening. "Yes, Dan," he said. "We did more than OK."

THURSDAY

The next morning at school, all Dan could think of was the tavern cellar and the wild, repulsive face of the loathsome speaker.

He was so freaked out about it that he tried chatting to his parents at breakfast to blot out the memory.

"You know you mentioned pizza and a movie the other day? Could we do it one night soon? This really good sci-fi film has just come out on DVD. Maybe we could borrow it from that shop on the high street?"

Dan noticed his parents exchanging a surprised look.

"Sounds good," replied his dad. "Let's do it on Saturday night."

***

During lunch break, Dan sat at the far end of the

playground near the main school gates. It was quiet over there and no one would disturb him. He needed some time to chill. He was just opening a running magazine when he saw the Golem standing by the gates, waving a hand at him.

"What are *you* doing here?" hissed Dan, running over to the gates.

"We're needed urgently," explained the Golem. "It can't wait."

Dan was about to ask what he should do about school but he could see from the Golem's expression that something *very* serious was going on. He looked around and quickly scaled one of the iron gates, landing with a thud on the pavement. The Golem was already off down the street. He was running from tree to tree, limiting the chances of someone spotting him. But the only person they passed was a young woman pushing a pram and she was wrapped up in a conversation with her gurgling baby.

The Golem's chest started to glow before they made it to the garage. A minute later, they flew inside and the light flash burst to life.

As the light vanished, Dan and the Golem saw that they were standing at the top of a hill, in the middle of some countryside. It was cold and dark and it was snowing. The only light came from the slim crescent moon hanging in the sky. Somewhere nearby, Dan could hear a loud commotion.

They found themselves looking down at a small village, nestled in the middle of a valley. There couldn't have been more than twenty houses, each one covered with thick snow. Dan's eyes were immediately drawn to a large, wooden building at the centre of the village. He saw a Star of David carved on to the building's front doors and realised instantly it was a synagogue. Outside the doors, a baying mob of ten men on horseback were hurling bricks and rocks at the side of the building. The men had swords resting against their legs.

"*Cossacks!*" hissed the Golem with contempt.

The Cossacks were shouting with excitement, their bodies pumped full of hatred and adrenaline. Several of the synagogue's windows had already been smashed, but they were too high for the Cossacks to climb through. So another, smaller group of five Cossacks were trying to force their way through the synagogue's heavy oak doors.

A noise from behind suddenly alerted Dan.

He spun round and in the distance saw a large group of people running in their direction. They held blazing torches, rocks and pieces of metal. One of them was carrying a ladder. They were obviously on their way to join the Cossacks.

"I'll deal with the newcomers," hissed the Golem urgently. "You go inside the synagogue."

Dan's heart crashed against his ribs in terror. "H... how am I going to do that?" he spluttered.

The Golem put a finger to his lips, grabbed Dan, lifted him over his shoulder and started running down the hill towards the synagogue. Dan felt his body bouncing as the Golem thundered forward. The Cossacks were so caught up in their attack that they failed to notice this huge creature and his human cargo, cutting round the back of the building.

"Good luck," whispered the Golem as he lifted Dan higher.

"What now?" asked Dan.

The Golem pulled Dan towards him and then hurled him through the air. Dan flew forwards. He held up his arms to protect his face, as he crashed through one of the synagogue's back windows. Shards of glass cascaded down all around him. He landed with a heavy thud but managed to roll sideways to break his fall.

In the dim light, he could make out a group of people who had taken shelter beneath four wooden trestle tables, on the left side of the synagogue. He hurried over and saw there were over fifty of them, men, women and children. They shrank back as Dan approached. He crouched down and held up his hands to show he wasn't carrying a weapon.

"I'm a friend," he said.

Some of the children held their hands over their eyes, afraid that Dan was about to hurt them.

"I'm here to help," Dan whispered.

Still they looked at him in terror.

Dan's mind was pulsating with fear. How did the Golem expect him to protect them? The Cossacks were armed; these people had no weapons. If the Cossacks broke through the front doors, everyone inside would be killed, including him. And where was the Golem?

At that second, there was a huge crash as a large piece of burning wood flew through one of the synagogue's front windows. It landed on top of a row of wooden benches. It was followed shortly by a second piece and then a third.

Dan scanned the room desperately. At the back of the building was a stage area with two large curtains hanging across the back of it. Beneath one of the curtains, he spotted a narrow door.

Where did it lead?

If it was just a way out of the back of the synagogue, it would be no use. The Cossacks would reach them within seconds. Dan had to find out, so he started running towards the door. As he ran, several bricks came raining down towards him, but he dodged out of their way.

Leaping on to the stage, he ran towards the narrow door and tried its handle.

It was locked.

He gave it a kick, but it stayed firmly shut. In

panic, he took a few steps back and then charged towards it. Using his left shoulder, he barged into the door and with a loud smack, it flew open. Dan peeked inside. It led to a small windowless antechamber, full of chairs and small square tables.

He turned back round. One of the synagogue's wooden benches had caught fire and the flames were slowly spreading down a row of seats.

Dan gulped and sprinted back towards the trestle tables. He stared at the flames anxiously. He had to get those people away!

"YOU HAVE TO COME WITH ME!" he yelled.

The people stayed where they were, shaking with terror.

"PLEASE!" shouted Dan desperately. "IF YOU DON'T, YOU'LL ALL BE KILLED!"

Something about Dan's urgent plea suddenly nudged the group into action. A few moments later they were crawling out from under the tables.

Dan ran back towards the antechamber, as stones and metal objects crashed through the windows. He quickly glanced over his shoulder and was relieved to see the whole party dashing after him. Dan flew into the antechamber and quickly ushered everyone inside.

He got to work immediately.

Slamming the narrow door shut, he grabbed some chairs and started building a barricade. He had to at least delay the Cossacks from getting to them. The others saw what he was doing and quickly joined in. In less than a minute they had constructed a deep blockade. There was a narrow crack in the door and Dan peered through it.

The flames were now licking their way across the synagogue's threadbare carpet towards the raised, central area of the synagogue – the *bimah*. Dan realised that staying inside this antechamber could only be a *very* temporary measure. If the Cossacks didn't get to them first, they'd all burn to death.

He wiped a strip of sweat off his forehead. Several of the men in the antechamber began chanting prayers. The smaller children clung to their mothers, the older ones shook with horror.

A couple of minutes later, with a mighty crash, the front doors of the synagogue finally gave way and Dan stared in terror as the Cossacks, now on foot, stormed into the building.

Panic shot through him.

Where was the Golem?

The Cossacks drew their swords and leapt over the flames in the direction of the antechamber. They scrambled up onto the stage and were only a couple of metres away from the antechamber door, when there was suddenly an ear-splitting roar from the front of the synagogue.

The Cossacks spun round in shock.

Amongst the flames, Dan could see the huge outline of the Golem storming inside and running towards the Cossacks. Three of them ran towards him, brandishing their long swords, but he punched them out of the way with his huge fists, as if they weighed no more than tennis balls.

The Golem roared as he stamped on

Dan made a snap decision. There were still twelve Cossacks on the stage. However strong the Golem was, he might not be able to take twelve of them on at the same time.

"He needs help!" shouted Dan, frantically

starting to pull at the chairs and tables blocking the door. Some of the men in the antechamber saw what he was doing and sprang to his assistance.

Suddenly they didn't look scared any more.

They looked angry.

As the last table was thrown out of the way, Dan and the men crashed out of the antechamber. The Cossacks were so busy staring at the Golem in terror, that they didn't turn round in time to face Dan and his allies. They reached the Cossacks at the same moment as the Golem. Dan and the men charged at the Cossacks, snatching their swords, and throwing them to the ground, while the Golem grabbed any he could lay his hands on and flung them across the synagogue's floor.

In a bundle of arms and legs and panic, the Cossacks limped and crawled to the front doors, beaten and traumatised. Two minutes later, Dan heard the sound of horses hooves retreating and finally fading into the distance.

At that second there was a commotion inside the synagogue. The women and children were pouring out of the antechamber, hugging their menfolk and sobbing with relief that they had all been spared. The women took off their shawls and aprons; the men took off their heavy coats. All of these garments were used to beat the flames.

As the fires in the synagogue were extinguished one by one, the slow clear-up operation began. Dan looked around for the Golem and spotted his silhouette just outside the synagogue's front doors. Dan slipped down an aisle, unnoticed, and joined his friend in the snow outside.

The Golem put a hand on Dan's shoulder. "You did well in there," he said solemnly.

"Thanks," Dan replied.

As they started tramping through the snow, away from the synagogue, Dan suddenly had a feeling that they were being followed. He spun round, expecting to see a Cossack or one of the village inhabitants behind them, but the path was empty.

Dan shrugged and at that moment he and the Golem were suddenly surrounded by a flash of piercing light. In an instant they found themselves back in the the Bernsteins' garage.

FRIDAY

Dan arrived at school, with the sights and sounds of the previous night still spinning through his brain. He could have been killed. They could have all been killed. But thanks to the Golem, the bravery of those around him, and his own quick thinking, a catastrophe had been averted – at least in that one particular situation. Dan shuddered. That scene had probably been repeated in hundreds of synagogues, terrifying thousands of innocent people. He shuddered.

The school day got off to a bad start, because the first thing Dan saw when he opened his locker was that his clay Golem model had been smashed to pieces. Its arms and legs and torso and head were unrecognisable broken fragments. A thin carpet of clay dust had settled on the floor of the locker.

Dan's heart plummeted. Not only was the model going to be the centrepiece of his presentation, he also felt that in some way it was protecting him – it was firmly linked to the Golem of Prague's appearance in his life. He tried to glue it together, but his Golem model was totally irreparable.

He noticed Lucy talking to someone a few metres away and slammed his locker door.

He thought about the smashed model all morning, and was still mulling it over when Steve Fenton and crew sidled up to him near the canteen in lunch break.

"Why did you smash it?" Dan asked angrily, jabbing a finger at Steve.

"Don't know what you're on about, *Bacon Boy,*" snapped Steve, giving Dan a shove in the chest.

"Yes, you do," hissed Dan.

Steve smirked at Tony and Gavin. "Prove it!"

"Just leave me alone!" said Dan, straightening up.

"Forget it," snarled Steve. "My uncle reckons that was all lies about your family being in debt. He says you must be hiding your money somewhere."

Dan raised his eyes to the heavens. "That's ridiculous," he snarled. "Why don't you come over after school today and pull up the floorboards. If you find a big stash down there, you can keep it."

Steve scowled.

Once again, Dan's comment had thrown him.

"Just shut it, *Bacon Boy*, and listen."

"What? To more rubbish?"

Steve grabbed Dan by the collar. "This is what's going to happen. Because you lot are so rich, I've decided that it's time you shared your money around."

"But I've already told you that..."

"Shut it!" snapped Steve. "Tomorrow at four o'clock, I want you to meet me at the back of the old brickworks by the canal. You bring me twenty pounds and I get off your case for a week."

"I don't have twenty pounds," replied Dan.

"No money and your face gets a makeover," hissed Steve. "Got it?"

Dan took a deep breath and nodded reluctantly.

Steve slapped him on the back. "Well done, *Bacon Boy*," he grinned, "and don't even think about not turning up. The punishment will be far worse if you don't show."

With that, Steve, Tony and Gavin walked off, laughing.

***

Dan sprinted home after school and made straight for the garage. The Golem was standing by the far wall. He looked deep in thought.

"The Steve Fenton thing's got worse," Dan panted. "He's asked me to pay him protection money – to keep him off my case. He's demanded twenty pounds. He told me to meet him behind the old brickworks tomorrow. If I don't have the cash, he said he'd batter me. What shall we do?"

The Golem sighed. "I have some bad news," he said.

Dan eyed him with suspicion.

"I won't be around tomorrow," said the Golem quietly. "We have worked well as a team. You have been very brave. But now it is time for me to go."

SATURDAY

Saturday dragged like a can of coke tied to the bumper of a slow-moving car. Dan checked his watch hundreds of times.

"Is anything wrong?" asked Mum, when she poked her head round his bedroom door just after two.

"No," he replied, "I'm just thinking."

"OK," she smiled, "I'll see you later then."

At quarter to four Dan set off.

He headed towards the canal and cut across the stretch of wasteland, rounded the corner and headed over to the old brickworks. Round the back was a large tarmac yard, with spindly weeds pushing out through the cracks and a burnt-out car lying on its side.

Steve was already there. Tony and Gavin were with him.

Dan took a deep breath and walked towards

them.

"Well done, *Bacon Boy*," called Steve. "Have you got the money?"

Dan walked over until he was only a couple of metres away from Steve. "No," he replied quietly. "I haven't got the money."

"Are you stupid or what?" hissed Steve, stepping towards him. "I said bring the money or you get a battering."

"I know what you said," replied Dan coolly, "and I told you I don't have it."

Steve glanced at his mates. The three of them looked uncertain. But Steve's face suddenly filled with angry resolve.

"You know what, *Bacon Boy*," he shouted, "I've had enough of you! Ever since you got here there's been a stench in this town. Everything was fine before Mr Jew arrived. But no, you come up here all flash as if you own the place. You think you can rule over normal British people like me. And that's not right. This is our country – not for Jews or blacks or any of those other ethnic minorities or whatever they call themselves. I reckon the whole lot of you should be put on ships and tipped into the middle of the ocean – that would be a result, wouldn't it, lads?"

Tony and Gavin giggled.

"Do you know what?" said Dan slowly. "You talk the biggest load of crap I've *ever* heard anyone spout. You qualify as the most ignorant, stupid specimen within a hundred mile radius. You're absolutely PATHETIC!"

Steve had clearly not been expecting this. His face dropped and he quickly looked at Tony and Gavin. They were also taken aback by Dan's outburst.

"Come on," snarled Dan. "Do you really think that if Jews were as rich and powerful as you and your uncle say we are, I'd be standing here having this conversation with you? I'd have paid some thugs to beat you up, wouldn't I? Face it, Steve, you're talking out of your backside."

This was a step too far for Steve. Without any warning he smashed his right fist towards Dan's head. The blow struck Dan on the forehead and floored him.

"GET UP, BACON BOY!" screamed Steve, his face purple with rage.

But before Dan could get to his feet, Steve kicked him in the ribs. Dan winced in pain.

"IT'S WHAT YOU DESERVE!" screamed Steve grabbing the collar of Dan's jacket and dragging him to his feet. "IT'S WHAT ALL FILTHY JEWS DESERVE!"

He pulled his fist back for another punch. But as the fist came smashing forwards, Dan struck out his right arm and blocked it.

Steve was totally shocked by this and he was even more startled when Dan punched him fiercely in the stomach.

Steve coughed and staggered back a few paces.

"THAT'S IT!" Steve bellowed. He charged towards Dan with both fists flailing. But Dan dived out of his way and gave him a good, hard kick on the back. Steve tottered forward a couple of steps and then thudded down, face-first on to the ground.

Dan was on him in a second. He yanked Steve's right arm and pulled it behind his back.

Steve yelped in agony. Dan knelt down until his face was only a few centimetres away from Steve's.

"Get off my arm!" pleaded Steve. "You're going to break it!"

Dan looked up and saw Tony and Gavin hovering nearby with terror on their faces. "Get out of here, you two!" commanded Dan.

They hesitated for a second.

"I SAID GO!"

They didn't need any further warnings. They turned and fled.

"Right," snarled Dan. "Let's just get a few things straight."

"I'll do whatever you want," whimpered Steve. "Please don't hurt me any more!"

"Listen carefully, Steve, and do everything I say."

"Number one, you stop spouting all of this racist rubbish – telling lies about Jews being rich and running the country and all of that stuff. And you lay off black and Asian people and anyone else who doesn't fit into your 'Whites Only' world."

"OK," sobbed Steve, "I'll stop it. I promise!"

"Number two, you stay well away from me.

No graffiti on pencil cases. No broken models. No demands for money. Do you get it?"

"Yes, YES!" replied Steve.

"And number three," hissed Dan, moving in even closer and whispering in Steve's ear. "Never, ever call me *Bacon Boy* again."

"I won't," cried Steve. "I'll never say it again. Please, please just let me go. I'll never even talk to you again."

Dan held his arm for another couple of seconds and then released it.

Steve scrambled across the ground, his face flushed beetroot with pain and tears. He struggled to his feet and ran away as best as he could.

Dan watched him until he'd vanished round a corner.

"Nice work," said a voice behind him.

Dan spun round in amazement.

It was Lucy's voice.

"What... what... are you doing here?" gasped Dan, seeing Lucy stepping out from behind a wall.

"I was just taking a walk round here when

I heard this commotion."

Dan gave her a funny look. "Yeah right," he said.

"OK," Lucy sighed. "I followed you."

Dan stared at her in surprise. "Why?"

"All this falling-out stuff between me and you is too teen drama."

Dan's face broke into a smile. "So you're not angry with me any more?" he asked.

She shook her head. "Do you still hate me?"

Dan blushed. "No… no… forget it."

"Well at least that's settled," grinned Lucy. "But there's a lot to talk about so we better get going. Your house or mine?"

MONDAY

Steve, Gavin and Tony sat in a miserable huddle at the back of the class on Monday morning. They all avoided eye contact with Dan.

Dan had spent all of Sunday round at Lucy's house. He'd come home very late, and told his parents he'd been doing an enormous piece of homework with her. They both gave him funny looks, but neither asked him any questions.

"Right," said Miss Foxton, "it's time to get cracking with the first of the presentations. Who wants to go first?"

A girl called Cara raised her hand. Her presentation was about a local girls' rugby team. She'd done it like a radio programme – with interviews and match reports and commentary. It was excellent.

"Great work, Cara," smiled Miss Foxton. "Who's next?"

A boy called Frank read some poems he'd done about his summer holiday on the Isle of Wight.

"Anyone else?" asked Miss Foxton, after congratulating Frank on his poems.

Dan and Lucy both raised their hands.

Miss Foxton looked puzzled. "Is this a joint presentation?"

They nodded.

"OK," she replied, "I didn't say anything about *not* doing joint presentations. What have you got for us?"

They walked together to the front of the class. Dan switched on the interactive whiteboard and slipped a disc into the class laptop.

Lucy dimmed the lights.

Then Dan pressed *play.*

Immediately the screen filled up with quick fire images of everyday school life; desks, chairs, coats and some kids playing football in the playground. Then suddenly it cut to a long-distance shot of some pencil cases lined up on a table. The camera moved along the row and then zoomed in on the last one.

It was Dan's, with the words DIRTY JEW scrawled across its front.

There were several gasps around the class.

Instantly this image disappeared and was replaced with some black-and-white footage of a young boy wearing a cardboard sign round his neck as three other boys threw stones at him. This scene took place in some sort of cemetery. A subtitle appeared on the screen – *France 1782*.

The film cut again, this time to the art cupboard. It panned over the shelves with their different materials and then showed a large pack of clay. A second later, the camera showed a locker being opened. Inside and clearly visible, were the smashed pieces of Dan's clay model.

Immediately after this, there followed a scene of several men on horseback, throwing bricks and chunks of wood through the smashed windows of a building. The camera panned round and the Star of David on the front door was very clear for all to see. A caption read, *Poland 1881*. Thick, dark wisps of smoke were wafting out of the synagogue.

Dan heard Miss Foxton's sharp intake of breath.

Next up was a moving shot, showing the towpath of a canal. The camera followed this path, took in a bridge and then turned the corner into the yard at the back of the old brickworks.

And there was Steve Fenton – swaggering around and yelling out his vicious anti-Semitic abuse, with Tony and Gavin in the background egging him on.

Dan glanced sideways and saw Miss Foxton putting her hand over her mouth.

Following Steve's vitriolic outburst, the film immediately cut to a smoky room, crowded with people. They were all facing a stage where someone was standing on a stage, addressing them. The words *Germany 1930* appeared on the screen.

The camera moved across the room until it focussed clearly on the speaker. There was no mistaking him. It was the same man Dan had come face-to-face with in the tavern's toilets.

It was Adolf Hitler.

He was in mid-rant, shouting and waving his arms around, his face alight with hatred and fury.

A shiver went round the entire class. Everyone

was absolutely stunned.

And then suddenly the screen went blank.

For over a minute no one spoke.

Lucy flicked a switch and people's eyes readjusted to the light. Everyone in the room turned to face Steve, Tony and Gavin, who were cowering at the back of the class. Steve was sobbing.

Miss Foxton glared at him furiously, her fists tightly clenched, her face apoplectic with rage.

She turned back to Dan. "Why...why didn't you tell me about all of this?" she asked quietly. "I would have acted immediately."

"I know that," nodded Dan, "but I just...I had to deal with it myself."

Miss Foxton nodded very slowly and pursed her lips; she was lost in thought. A few moments later she composed herself and a look of steely determination spread across her face.

"Right," she said, looking up at her class. "It's break time in two minutes. Until then, I want everyone to sit quietly and think about Dan and Lucy's incredibly powerful film. I'm sure you'll all agree, it shows very clearly how small acts of racism and hatred can pave the way for far more devastating episodes."

Two minutes later, the class filed out silently.

Miss Foxton kept back Dan, Lucy, Steve, Gavin and Tony.

"Right, you three," she said, "go straight to the head teacher's office. I'll meet you there in five minutes."

Steve, Tony and Gavin shuffled out, each gazing down at the floor miserably. They looked very scared.

Miss Foxton took a deep breath. "I'm bowled over by your bravery and determination, Dan," she said, "and by your vital assistance in this project, Lucy."

The three of them were silent for a moment.

"There's something that's intriguing me though about the historical scenes," said Miss Foxton eventually.

Dan and Lucy exchanged a glance.

"Now I'm no expert on film making," she said, "but I do know that you couldn't buy a camcorder in France in 1782; likewise Poland in 1881. And although I've seen many programmes about Adolf Hitler and the rise of Nazism, I have never, ever, seen any footage that was shot so clearly and in such good colour. Am I missing something here?"

Dan cleared his throat. His answer was well prepared. "We found this amazing web site that has millions of historical images," he explained. "They've developed this technology that can recreate scenes from the past and turn them into colour films that look incredibly contemporary. So we can't take credit for those historical scenes because someone else put them together."

"Can anyone gain access to the site?" asked Miss Foxton with interest.

Lucy shook her head. "It's subscription only and costs hundreds of pounds to join. My dad's a member – that's how we got onto it."

"Fascinating," murmured Miss Foxton. "Today's technology amazes me more and more every day. May I borrow the disc?" she enquired. "I'd like the head teacher to see it."

"Sure," Dan replied. He walked over to the

laptop, ejected the disc and handed it over.

"Thank you," smiled Miss Foxton. "I still wish you'd come to me earlier about this appalling situation. Rest assured that Steve and his friends will be firmly dealt with. Now I suggest you two go outside and get some fresh air before break ends."

***

A couple of minutes later, Dan and Lucy were sitting on a bench in the playground.

"I can't believe you managed to film all of those scenes," Dan said.

"I was furious with you when you shouted at me on Tuesday afternoon," said Lucy. "But I knew that something really big was about to kick off and I wasn't going to miss it. So I followed you and snuck into the garage. I was swept up with you and the Golem and landed up outside that graveyard, a few metres away from you. I ducked and hid and then filmed the scene with my dad's camcorder."

Dan remembered the movement he'd spotted outside the graveyard. He'd thought it was a dog or another animal, but it had been Lucy!

"After that, there was no way I was going to miss any other bits of action," she added, "so I crept in there after you on Wednesday and Thursday as well."

Suddenly the figure disappearing through the bar door and the sense of being followed outside the synagogue made complete sense: Lucy again.

Dan shook his head and smiled. "And you broke into my locker and found the pencil case and the broken model?"

"It wasn't really breaking in," she grinned, "I just used a ruler to twist the screw. I could see you were hiding something in there so I wanted to film that as well."

"We really freaked out Miss Foxton, didn't we?" Dan said.

"We really freaked out ourselves," Lucy replied, "especially in that tavern."

Dan shivered. "I still can't believe I came face-to-face with Hitler. It was my absolute worst nightmare."

"I know," nodded Lucy. "I'm just so upset that the Golem isn't able to *change* the course of history.

If he had that power, he'd be able to save millions and millions of lives."

They sat in silence for a while.

"So how long did you spend with the Golem on Friday night?" asked Lucy finally. "You know after he told you he was leaving – when he showed you the fight moves?"

"Ages," Dan replied. "It must have been about three hours. He was a brilliant teacher though, and he didn't leave until I'd really mastered them. He said preparation is everything. Without him, I'd have definitely been beaten by Steve."

Lucy paused for a few moments. "What do you think they'll do with Steve?" she eventually asked.

Dan shrugged his shoulders. "By the way Miss Foxton looked, I reckon they'll come down on him like a collapsing brick wall."

***

By lunchtime everyone in the school had heard about the film and Steve's repulsive behaviour. Loads of kids approached Dan and told him how disgusted they were with Steve and many of them praised the way Dan had taken him and his henchmen on. Shortly after this, rumours about Steve's punishment flew around the school. Some people said Steve had been taken away in a police van, others claimed the story would be on the front page of a national newspaper the next day.

Miss Foxton told the class that Tony and Gavin had been excluded for a month, while Steve had been expelled. Dan thought about Steve's uncle for a second. In spite of his mad theories and position as a local councillor, there was no way he'd have the power to reinstate his nephew at the school.

Dan got the feeling that Miss Foxton didn't think expulsion was a harsh enough punishment for Steve, but she kept her own counsel and got on with the next lesson.

***

That night, Dan and Lucy went into Dan's garage so that they could talk without Dan's parents overhearing them. As they opened the door, they immediately saw a silhouetted figure hovering by the upturned crates.

"The Golem's back," whispered Lucy.

But when they closed the door and switched on the light, they saw that their visitor was not the Golem. It was an elderly man with white hair and a long white beard; the man Dan had seen by the river.

"Rabbi Loeb?" asked Dan, hesitantly.

"You must be Dan," nodded the Rabbi, "and I take it this is Lucy?"

They nodded.

"I'm sorry, but the Golem can't be with me tonight," explained the Rabbi. "We have our own problems in Prague." He sighed. "You have learnt some vital lessons in the past few days," he said softly. "But I want to remind you that it is imperative, *at all times,* to follow the path of peace. You must strain every sinew in your body to find a peaceful solution to any given problem – however intractable it may seem. Discuss, debate, reason. Talking has saved many lives. It is a far more powerful weapon than many people imagine. But if you have used up every possible peaceful solution and you are faced with physical assault – then talking will not get you out of trouble. One of the greatest lessons of history is that if you are attacked, you *must* fight back if it is possible. It is not only your right as a human being, it is your duty. If the gun and the sword are the only language your detractors' understand, then you must be prepared to battle for your life."

Dan and Lucy's eyes were fixed intently on Rabbi Loeb.

"Furthermore," the rabbi added. "If a group of people are attacked and you are an *onlooker*, you *must* step in to protect this group and do whatever it takes to end the violence against them."

Dan and Lucy nodded together.

"These rules do not apply just to Jews," said Rabbi Loeb. "We are not the only group who have had the spotlight of racism and intolerance upon us. In Bosnia, in Rwanda, in Darfur, the vulnerable have been attacked mercilessly. When the attacked are not strong enough to defend themselves – the onlooking world must step in and stamp on these outrages as soon as possible. The saving of human lives comes above all else."

"It must be shocking for you to see these terrible things repeated again and again," whispered Dan.

Rabbi Loeb smiled sadly. "Yes Dan, it is shocking and extremely painful. One of the human race's worst crimes is not to learn these vital lessons of history. I pray that in your own lives, terrible events such as these will become more rare. And while your experience with Steve Fenton was nothing like any of the others I have mentioned, it was still deeply unpleasant. I am very proud of the way you both acted."

"So what happens now?" asked Dan.

The Rabbi took a deep breath. "It is time for me to return to my world," he said. "Prague in 1580 is not such a great place for a Jew to live. There are forces agitating against my community and I need to be there with them. In between his leaps into history, my Golem has much work to do."

"Will he ever come back and will..?"

But before Dan's question was complete, the legendary Rabbi of Prague had vanished.

TUESDAY

The following morning, Dan whistled to himself as he poured some cereal into a bowl.

"You seem cheerful," noted Mum, coming into the kitchen and looking for the paper.

Dan looked up and grinned.

"Is it something to do with running?" Mum enquired.

Dan shook his head.

Mum tousled his hair and reached for a loaf of bread.

***

Just before registration, Dan and Lucy were chatting by the lockers.

"Now it's all over," said Lucy, "what's our next project?"

"It won't be anything like our last one," Dan smiled.

Lucy laughed. "Well I'm going to finish my snake movie," she declared. "I'm filming at the zoo on Saturday – you can come if you want."

"Sure," Dan nodded, "that would be good."

"What about you?" Lucy asked, "Are you still furious with your parents?"

Dan laughed. "I'm being a bit easier on them. I overheard Mum telling Dad that she might only be able to stand a year at this new job."

Lucy frowned. "Well *I* don't want you to go back to London after just a year."

Dan sighed. "Anyway, this morning I saw my dad using this great new glue for all of these jobs round our house. I'm going to use it to fix my Golem model."

"Cool," said Lucy, "and if it doesn't work you could make a new one."

Dan pulled a face. "Er… no. I think it's a one-off."

Lucy gave Dan a friendly thump on the arm and she headed off towards their class.

Dan hung back. He pulled out his key ring and opened his locker. Moving several scraps of paper out of the way, he reached for the shattered pieces of his Golem model. But to his amazement, he didn't feel any broken bits of clay. Instead, his fingers curled round the whole model. It was complete and smooth, just like it had been after it had been fired in the kiln.

Dan gazed at his rebuilt clay man with utter disbelief.

He lifted it up to inspect it more carefully, and as he did so, for a split second, from the centre of the Golem's chest, came a distant, orangey/yellow glow.

JONNY ZUCKER always wanted to be an
author and wrote lots of stories while at school.
He trained as a teacher and supplemented his teaching
income by writing part-time, composing songs for a
children's theatre company and doing stand-up comedy
gigs in the evenings. Eventually he started to write
full-time and has now written over thirty books for
children, teenagers and adults. These include the
Venus Spring and *Max Flash* series and *James, King
of England*. Jonny regularly appears at book festivals
and leads writing workshops in schools.
He lives in London with his family.